D1514873

THERE'S A FLY ON MY TOAST!

Poems by Justin Matott
Drawings by John Woods, Jr.

CLOVE PUBLICATIONS, INC.
Here.   There.   Everywhere.

For Andy, my wise and wonderful word warden.
For Snickers, Tootsie Roll and Baby Ruth for naming this book.
For JJ and Ethan, for constantly filling my head with ideas to write about.
—JM

For John, David and Melissa.
—JW

A special thank you to Herb Allison for his "designing ways,"
and to all of the wonderful teachers, media specialists, and students we've met
along the way, especially Cougar Run Elementary teachers, Emily Berg,
Kim McMonagle and Nicole DiPasquale!

THERE'S A FLY ON MY TOAST
Text copyright © 2003 by Justin Matott
Illustrations copyright © 2003 by John Woods, Jr.

Library of Congress Cataloging-in-Publication Data
There's a Fly on My Toast written by Justin Matott;
illustrated by John Woods, Jr. – 1st ed. p. cm.
Summary: Assorted quips and poems about the everyday stuff of life.
ISBN 1-889191-23-X   {1. poetry. I. John Woods, Jr. 1954— ill. II. Title

First edition
Second Printing
Printed in China
To contact Mr. Matott regarding his work, please write to
Clove·Publications, Inc., or email him in care of RandomWrtr@aol.com.
For Mr. Woods, please email: jwoodsjr@tlnk.com.

THERE'S A FLY ON MY TOAST!

WELCOME, COME ON IN

Welcome to my house of words!
Welcome to this place!
My goal within, to make you think,
or put a smile upon your face.

The subjects here all vary,
the thoughts are random, too.
I hope you like this book a lot!
Oh boy, I hope you do!

So welcome now my newest friend.
Please get a comfy chair.
And read and read and read and read,
for now, have not a care…

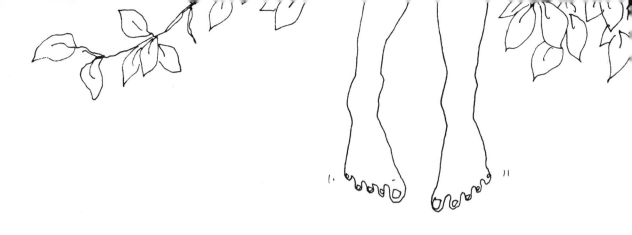

MY TREEHOUSE

I go there when I'm happy.
I go there when I'm sad.
I like to climb right up my tree,
it makes me really glad!

And when I find myself alone,
in my tree house all to me,
I take my shoes and socks off,
and let my toes go free.

JELLO'S IN MY NOSE

Jello squirted from my nose,
my friend just said a funny.
Went in my mouth all wiggly,
came out my nose all runny.

I know that sounds disgusting.
But it's also kind of great!
Next time I'll use a GIANT bowl,
it slips right off my plate!

9

A BOY I KNEW ONCE

I knew this little boy back when.
Had hair that stood straight out.
He had a funny, froggy voice,
it sounded like a SHOUT!

One leg was shorter than the other,
on one eye he wore a patch.
That little boy was really shy,
his clothes would never match!

Then one day he began to grow,
both legs stretched out the same.
The patch came off his eye,
and his voice began to tame.

His confidence began to grow!
"YOU ALL JUST WAIT AND SEE!"
How did I know this little boy?
That little boy was me!

LUNCHROOM LADY BLUES

Our lunchroom ladies are uptight!
They never let us play!
"You cannot have a food fight!
Save it for your weekend day!"

But when their backs are turned,
we throw our lunch around.
They spin about so quickly,
to try to find the sound.

The place from where a sandwich flew,
is what they must explore,
and when they turn their backs again,
we throw a couple more.

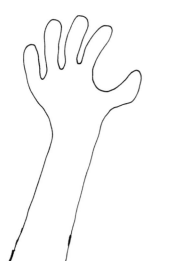

SCHOOL LUNCH

School lunch is made with paper towels,
the pizza dough with glue.
Other art supplies are added,
but the rest? I have no clue.

The lunch ladies are all sneaky!
I bet they're truly spies!
I'm sure my apple cobbler
is really filled with flies.

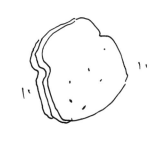

A SON

A son is his dad's mirror,
of his actions and his words.
When Dad starts acting goofy,
his son, too, acts absurd.

Sons do just what their dads do,
not only what they say.
They watch them very closely,
all night and every day.

WHAT?

What's that you just said?
"**What**" is a wondrous word.
What starts me imagining
things some think absurd.

What? Is a way to start a thought.
Don't forget a question mark.
What is a very special word!
To make your thinking spark.

SALT AND PEPPER

I asked only for the salt,
was handed pepper, too.
I don't understand just why,
someone give me a clue.
No matter who you ask,
to pass the salt, it's true.
They'll hand it with the pepper,
they always come in twos.
They seem to go together,
salt and pepper are a match.
Why can't you ever find them,
grown in a salt and pepper patch?

DON'T RAIN ON MY PARADE

I wish it was always sunny,
so a parade would come each day!
I want one in December,
but I'll have to wait 'til May.

MY DOG'S BOW TIE

I got my dog a bow tie,
I think he looks well dressed.
I like to help him make believe.
Next came his dashing vest!

Tried on my dad's best hat,
pulled down low on his eye.
When Dad saw him wearing it,
he laughed, said he looked sly.

And then he pulls on trousers,
to make his look complete.
Soon he'll want four fancy shoes,
to wear down on his feet.

Oh, he's fearless and he's daring,
dressed like a private eye.
I got my dog a bow tie,
and now you know just why!

WHEN BOYS PLAY

When boys play cops and robbers,
or when they go to war,
they carry brooms and tools,
and fight across the floor.

But never say they're "playing,"
to them they're *in* the battle.
And never tell their secret codes,
real warriors never tattle.

If you act like they are playing,
or say it's just pretend,
your suit of armor better work,
for your castle you'll defend.

They'll turn against you in their war,
a traitor to take down!
Just tell them they're the real thing,
then a smile will turn their frown.

CONNECTING ALL MY FRECKLES

I once drew a tiny line,
from one freckle to the next.
My whole face got lined up,
my dad got very vexed!

"Vexed" means kind of mad.
Though I'm not sure just why.
"It's my face!" I said loudly,
as Dad let out a sigh.

YOU'LL SEE SOMEDAY

I'm going to have a bunch of dogs,
when I grow up, you'll see!
They'll live all about my house,
with my horses and monkey!

I want to have all kinds of pets.
And someday I just will!
Mom says one dog is quite enough,
but my whole house they'll fill!

I'll have more than the circus!
I'll have more than the zoo!
"When it is my own house,
then that is what I'll do."

WHAT SHOELACES DO

My shoelaces lace to keep my feet in.
When they get untied, then I start to grin.
My tootsies can move, now they can breathe.
I'll remove my shoelaces soon, I believe.

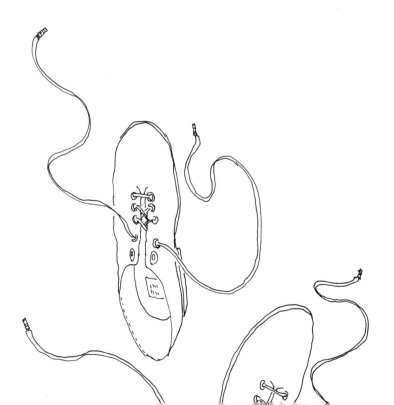

FLY AWAY NOW!

There's a black fly near my breakfast. He is really gross!
I don't like him here or there! I think he's way too close!
So, I got out my fly swatter, I raised it up so high.
That ugly, old buggy thing, lifted way off to the sky.
I heard him up there buzzing, all over my whole place,
driving me so crazy, he was invading all my space.

And just when I had spied him, was ready to go SMASH,
my cat started meowing, then I heard a SPLASH!
She jumped into a full sink, and YOWLED out really loud.
The fly was meanly smirking, he seemed so very proud.
My dog next got into the act, she growled at that bad fly.
If she ever got hold of him, that fly would surely die.

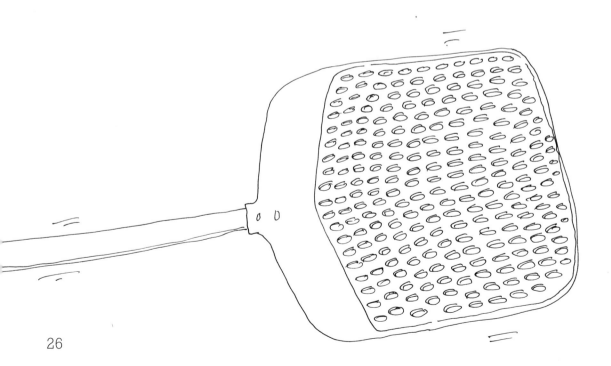

He popped up, she barked and leaped into the air,
that fly flew away so lazily, he didn't seem to care.
When all seemed quite hopeless, in walked my little brother.
He wondered what had caused the fuss, was ready to tell Mother.
We watched that fly go buzzing, then he whispered just to me,
"You think that this is hard? Try fighting a small flea."

He picked up father's newspaper, then he shouted "THERE!"
And jumped up on his tiptoes, and leaped up in the air.
With one half-hearted swat, he brought that big fly down.
But he hadn't killed him and that just made him frown.
I tied a thread to that noisy fly, and put him on a leash.
We named him Grizwaldo Von Stewart - his favorite food is quiche.

T-BONES AND EGGS FOR BREAKFAST

My grandpa makes big breakfasts.
Stuff mom just makes for dinner.
But, it tastes good in the morning.
Grandpa's breakfasts are a winner!

HAVING CHINESE TO GO

I like to eat it spicy,
when it comes all in a box!
The small cardboard container,
thrills me right out of my socks!

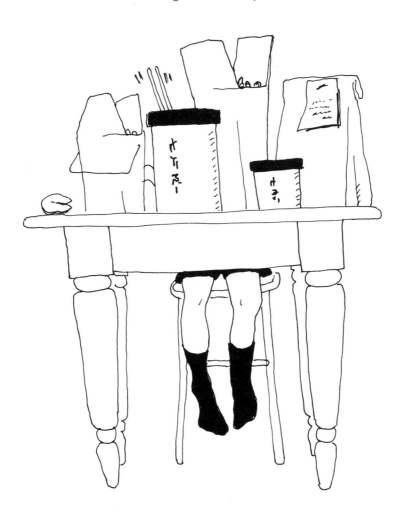

THE MYSTERY WHISTLER

At night when alone in my bed,
I heard a noise so weird.
It woke me up and scared me,
these things I've always feared.
It's mournful and it's kind of sad,
and has a haunting tune.
It came from somewhere in my house,
I must go find it soon.

I just pushed deeper down,
to the bottom of my bed.
But, I couldn't get that whistling noise
out of my poor head.
Yes, downstairs someone's whistling,
a tune I've never heard.
It sounds just like a sad, sad song…
a tune, oh so absurd.

I ventured down the stairs,
to see what I could see.
It's coming from the laundry room,
then it occurred to me.
The whistling had a familiar sound,
a loud breathing, then a sigh.
Suspecting who was in there,
still afraid to go close by.

As I crept up to the laundry room,
it sounded like a crowd.
I tiptoed in to see the source,
then I just laughed out loud.
Twitching with the nostril music
was my big old doggy Rover.
His nose was whistling loudly,
I told him to roll on over.

A BONE IN MY GARDEN

I found a dinosaur bone,
as I planted a flower.
I imagined his MASSIVE roar,
and his AWESOME power.

Was it part of his front leg?
Was it part of a back claw?
I wondered if it might be
the hook of his GREAT jaw?

He once roamed my backyard,
oh now so long ago.
If he was still around,
I'd have a dino show!

OH, PLEASE MAY I DRIVE?

It looks like so much fun, the way the wheel moves.
I want to drive right now, in the ruts and in the grooves.
But, I can't see over the wheel and my feet don't reach the floor.
I'll just have to wait, for a decade, maybe more.

MY OLD TEDDY BEAR

He's now on my shelf, he used to be on my bed.
We would curl up close at night, him right near my head.

But, of course I am too old, for Teddy toys and such.
Who am I trying to kid? Yes, I love him, oh so much!

Now he's back in my bed, and again I'm sleeping well.
All my dreams, when I wake up, to Teddy I will tell.

MY OWN PILLOW

It puffs and billows!
It fluffs just right!
I like my pillow best!
Oh, I wish I had a thousand pillows,
when I put my head to rest.

IMAGINE THAT

I'm alone! I'm alone! Oh, what shall I do?
I could read or just play, my story is true!

I'm lost in the jungle, on this island remote.
So far from the city, wish I had a boat!

Out here on my island, I am so alone.
What's that strange sound? I think it's my phone!

I am back in my bedroom, well, I never was gone.
My imagination's keen, now there's a bear on my lawn.

I'll go out and wrestle him, but there is one hitch.
There's a really large rhino, hiding out in our ditch!

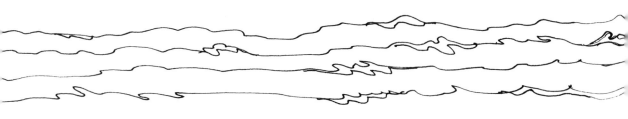

NIGHTMARES

In the middle of the night
my dreams are really scary!
The monster underneath my bed
is bunchy and all hairy!

But when I looked real close at him
I saw just what he was.
He's simply my own skivies.
And he's there just because.

Mom wanted my room clean, so
I shoved my clothes down there.
That monster's really nothing,
but my scary underwear.

CLOWNS

With brightly colored faces,
and hair all up in orange,
the clowns they entertain us,
but nothing rhymes with orange.

MY BLANKET, MY BED

There's no other place, I think of as great…
than my very own bed, always comfy, first rate!
I like burrowing down, inside of this cave.
My blankets, my bed, of it I must rave!

CHEESEBURGERS

For breakfast or dinner or even for lunch!
I'll eat them forever, munch them by the bunch!
I like it when they're double!
I like some extra cheese!
Cheeseburgers are awesome!
I'll have two, pretty please!

THE DOGHOUSE

Dad said we're in trouble. We forgot to clean our mess.
Mom came home and found it, and she's now really stressed.

Now Dad and I are camping, in our backyard it would seem.
"Move over, little Rover. Yes, we'll keep your doghouse clean!"

POEM OR NO POEM

Sometimes they all rhyme,
a poem is what I mean.
Sometimes they just don't,
carrot doesn't rhyme with bean.

That doesn't make a bit of sense,
you think up in your head.
This should have been a "No poem, poem."
I'll write a different one instead...

GOODNIGHT MY LITTLE BROTHER

"Good morning" is, the way we started.
Soon midday came and then we parted.
We said, "Good day," when you came back,
and then at night we yelled, "ATTACK!"

Our pillow fight began.
You swung hard, I just ran.
Then came the time to say goodnight,
at the end of a really great pillow fight!

You are my brother.
You are the greatest.
But, I am older,
I stay up latest.

Stay in bed now little brother,
or Mom will get upset.
It isn't morning, it's still dark.
Don't try to get up yet!

Goodnight, Goodnight,
Goodnight, Goodnight.
Okay, one more pillow fight!

A BOOK AT NIGHT

I like to sit up reading,
with my lamp into the night.
When I read my scary stories,
I use an extra light.

And sometimes it's a mystery,
that clutches me 'til late.
I want to know who done it,
I think that's really great!

When I read a funny little book,
I laugh into my pillow.
If the book is kind of humorous,
my laughter starts to billow!

And soon there will be knocking,
on that side of my door.
I wonder if it's my mother,
or my brother who is bored.

He hears me in here giggling,
or maybe hears my fear.
I wonder if he'll venture in,
to see me reading here.

When in my room a story comes,
to visit me 'til late.
There's nothing like a favorite book.
It is always very great!

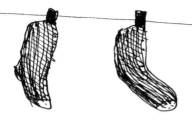

MY SHORTS ARE TIGHT

My undershorts are too tight,
they're giving me a goose!
They bunch up and they bug me,
so tight on my caboose.

Now I have a major wedgy,
from my shorts, I'll tell my mother.
Then I noticed they aren't mine,
they're from my little brother.

MY STREETLIGHT

Outside of my window
is a light, oh so bright!
Burns all the night long,
chasing away all my fright!

Night beasties stay away,
when the streetlight's so bright.
I hope it never goes off,
least not during the night.

THE GIGGLES

One morning as I sat in church,
something hit me kind of funny.
I chuckled low into my hand,
then my nose got really runny.

And soon my shoulders wiggled,
and my stomach got so tight.
I would burst if I held it in,
and any longer I just might.

Then the funniest thing happened.
A snort from Daddy's nose.
He, too, thought it funny,
as his laughter sort of rose.

Then the man with a hardened face,
right next to my dear mother,
did something unexpected,
he elbowed my dumb brother.

The two of them soon were howling,
then the whole church joined on in.
And on the pastor's face up front,
I thought I saw a grin.

His wife sat in the front row,
she let out a big guffaw.
The pastor started laughing hard,
and that's just what I saw.

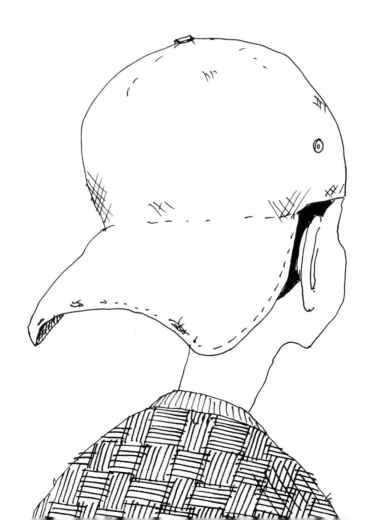

MY FAVORITE HAT

I sometimes wear it backwards,
with the bill just pointing back.
I sometimes turn it sideways,
I look like I should quack!

FUNNY IDEAS

I get some funny ideas.
Sometimes they float away.
I forget to write them in my book,
to save for another day.

I wish I could remember,
the one I thought of last.
I didn't write it down though,
and now it's in my past.

ROSES SCHMOSES

Roses are red,
violets are blue,
this book's black and white,
so that'll have to do.

I WATCHED A SPIDER

I watched a spider in her web,
and wondered what she saw.
She spun and spun the thin clear lines,
to catch flies in her claw.

The song she sang to lure them in
sounded really sweet and low.
I thought the bugs would find her out,
when they came to her show.

But, they all flew into her web
and got all stuck and bound.
I watched that little spider,
spin her web down to the ground.

RAINING CATS AND DOGS

It's raining cats and dogs out there,
they're pouring from the sky.
It seems so strange to see that,
I'm wondering just why?

What makes the doggies fall so fast?
What makes those kitties drop?
Maybe they were playing chase,
and then just couldn't stop.

THE GUESTROOM

My aunt is in the guestroom,
now it's smelling really bad.
I tattled to my mom,
and then I told my dad.

What is that she's using
that makes such an awful stench?
It's her very best perfume,
smells like a rose and wrench.

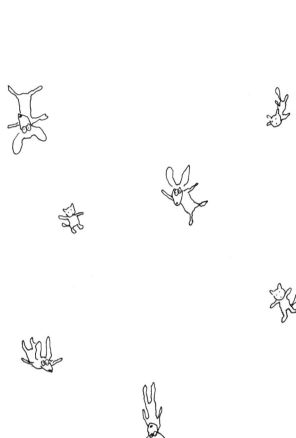

CHORES = SNORES

On Mondays it's my turn to clean,
the schedule Mom has goes.
On Tuesdays, I take out the trash,
decide what stays or throws!

Then Wednesdays, I must do the wash,
and fold it up just right.
Thursdays are my biggest days,
I do my chores all night!

Friday comes with its own work,
it seems to never end.
But Saturdays, when I want to play,
my help I'll surely lend.

When Sunday comes along I rest,
or just go out to play.
Yet when I think my chores are done
here comes good old Monday.

TURN OFF THOSE LIGHTS

Why is it only Dad knows how,
to turn the lights off right?
When you leave the room and don't
he always gets uptight!

Dad follows everyone around,
and grumbles about waste.
He says, "Turn off those lights my son,
my daughter, make some haste!"

For when you leave the room,
you must learn to turn them out!
"Those lights cost us some money.
Don't make me have to shout!"

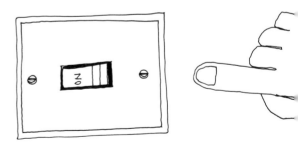

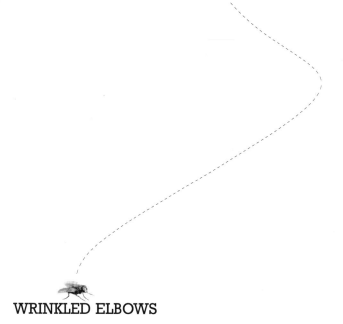

WRINKLED ELBOWS

Where do the wrinkles go, when I push out my wrist?
Why does my elbow pucker, when I punch out my fist?

And my knees get all scrunchy, as I straighten out my leg.
These are the wrinkly questions, and for answers I now beg.

Where do elbow wrinkles go, when they aren't on show right here?
Where do they go? I wonder, where do they go?

Oh dear…

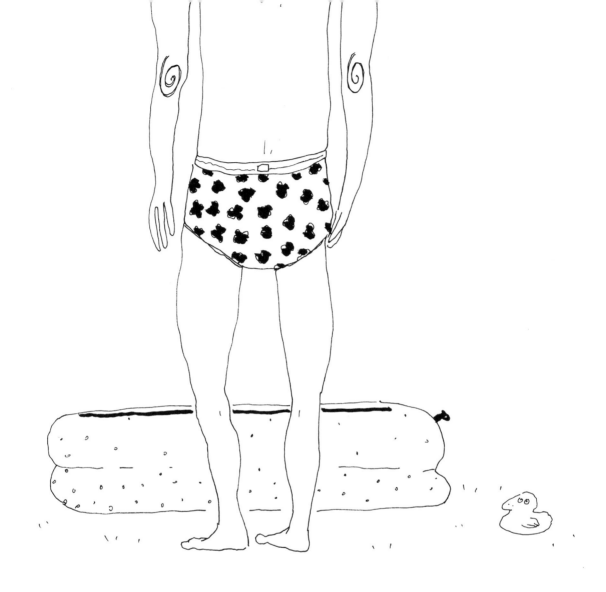

WHY DO I SNORT WHEN I LAUGH?

When I find something funny,
I chortle and I giggle.
I make some really funny sounds,
my throat then starts to wiggle.

Not snickering exactly,
no nothing of that sort.
When I laugh out loud quite hard,
I give out a REAL BIG SNORT!

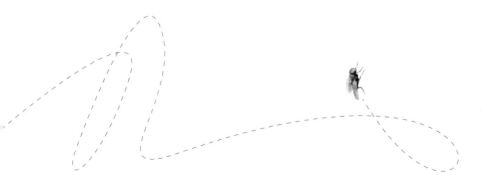

NOT ALL IT'S CRACKED UP TO BE

When I look at my bottom in the mirror,
I notice it's cracked up.

Did someone sometime drop me,
when I was just a pup?

My bottom is nicely padded,
so I'm comfortable when I sit.

My bottom just cracks me up,
and that's all there is to it!

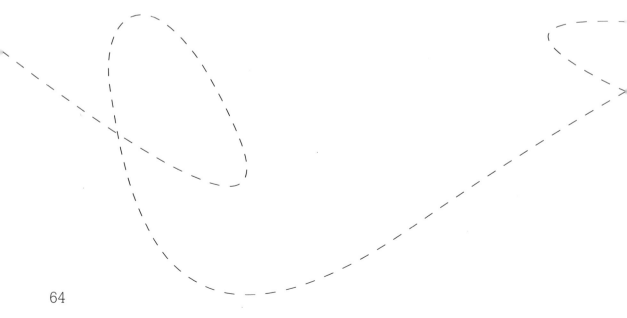

THERE'S A FLY ON MY TOAST!

This morning as I ate my breakfast,
something happened I must tell.
There was some bacon frying,
and the eggs smelled really swell!

But the greatest part of morning,
is my favorite raisin toast!
I asked for extra pieces,
I like that toast the most!

My momma brought it to me,
and set it on the table.
I looked at all that breakfast,
and wondered was I able?

So much to eat for little old me!
How could I do it? You wait and see!

Then I wanted some good jelly,
so I went back to the shelf.
And when I came back gasping,
I spilled it on myself.

Right there on my favorite toast
was an enormous, ugly fly.
Munching on my breakfast,
as I began to cry.

"MOMMA, THIS IS REALLY AWFUL!"
Looked like I'd seen a ghost.
"I cannot eat my breakfast now!
THERE'S FLY POOP ON MY TOAST!"

FISH BONES AND FRANKS

Fish bones and franks,
is a dinner for cranks.
Made of hog guts and slimy fish eyes,
I mix it in well. My brother says, "SWELL!"
Someday I'll tell him my little surprise.

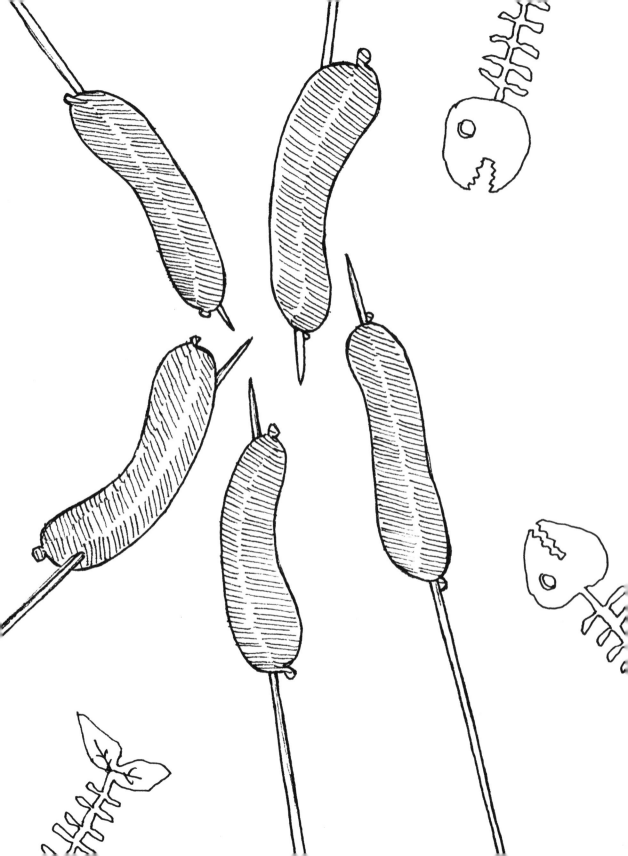

THE POEM I COULDN'T FINISH

I once had a thought,
which couldn't be bought
for all of the world's China tea!

I knew it was funny,
and witty and punny,
but it was only amusing to me.

When I tried to share it,
no one else could bear it,
so, I just let this half-poem be.

A REALLY BAD POEM

This poem is going to be SO bad,
I'll warn you from the start.
My brother likes to rhyme his words
so they all sound like… gas.

He tells me to write some stuff
to make Mom's face droop.
He likes to use words, which describe
another word for… doo-doo.

And nostril stuff he thinks so funny,
and over words we've fought.
Like when you blow your nose too hard,
and blow out all your… tissues.

I never understand his point,
he says kids like those words.
He says his all-time favorite though,
is a huge pile of dog… (well, you know).

He's always tried to get me to write
words to describe *HIS* awful stuff.
You aren't supposed to say it though,
so we'll just say, "Oh, fluff."

CONVERSATIONS WITH ECHO

While walking and out hiking
on a trail right down the way
I found my friend the Echo
when he came out to play.
I called out to him

                       then he called me back.
I said, "HEY, HELLO!"

                       No time did he lack,
"HEY, HELLO" to you, too!

                       He called down my way.
I said, "HOW ARE YOU?"

                       "HOW ARE YOU?" he would say.
He's seems just like my sister,

                       who repeats what I've just said.
Sometimes it's amusing

                       sometimes it's what I dread.
"WHERE ARE YOU?" I yelled.

                       And stood awaiting an answer.
"WHERE ARE YOU?" he replied.

                       Oh, this guy was a dancer.
"JUST *ANSWER* ME, MISTER,"

                       I yelled right down the way.
"JUST ANSWER *ME,* MISTER,"

                       he yelled back on that day.
I grew so tired of all his games,

                       so I yelled, "GO AWAY!"
And I bet you can guess

                       what Echo then did say.
I said, "OH HURUMPH!"

                       And then said, "POOH."
A "hurumph" and a "pooh"

                       came from echo, too.
I turned and resolved
I had said all I would.
Echo said nothing else,
I thought that was good.

THE BOOGEYMAN

Mom and Dad say he's not real
so what is in the dark?
I've seen him in my room at night.
I saw him in the park.

He's scary like a vampire guy,
in the corner of my room.
But only when it's dark I'd say,
which always comes too soon.

I imagine him in my closet,
and then under my bed.
I will glance that way just once,
and see his ugly head.

He follows me around at times,
just as does the moon.
I'll jump out brave and scream, "BOO!"
Oh, I will so very soon.

But right now I'm deep under cover,
at the very bottom of my bed.
Maybe if I stay right here,
he'll bug my sis instead.

EAT YOUR OATMEAL

"I want bacon and eggs!
And a pile of raisin toast!"
I yelled loud at my mother.
"THAT'S A BREAKFAST I LIKE MOST!"

Mom gave me a sharp look,
to settle me right down.
"EAT YOUR OATMEAL!" she growled,
with a really big mom frown.

"EAT YOUR OATMEAL!" she'd said,
and then let out a sigh.
To myself I said, "I won't!
I think I'd rather die!"

"There are children who are starving,
who would be happy to eat that!"
So I packaged it all up
in a parcel, big and fat.

I took it to the mailbox,
marked -WHOEVER WANTS TO EAT-
My oatmeal, it's so, so gross,
I'd rather have a treat.

As I turned from the mailbox,
my mom was standing there,
with her hands upon her hips,
and a really mean mom stare.

I pulled the package back out,
which now was cold and sticky!
And with each nasty bite,
I snarled, "MOM, THIS IS SO ICKY!"

I SCRATCH MY DOGGY'S FLEAS

When I tickle on her tummy,
try to help her scratch her fleas.
My doggy just smiles and smiles,
and kicks up both her knees.

Her leg then starts a'moving,
in a pace with all my itching.
My little dog's whole body,
just starts to go a'twitching.

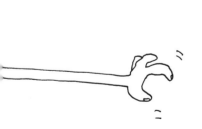

PET THE DOG

Go and pet a dog.
See what that will do.
It makes you grow calmer.
Brings out a better YOU!

Dogs have all the answers,
they are friendly and sincere.
Go and pet a little dog,
or a big one, do you hear?

When you pet a dog,
it's calming just because.
Go and pet a doggy now,
and see just what that does.

GAS STATION BATHROOMS

The key's as huge as Texas,
with a chain as big as France.
If I hold the gas station key,
I can't undo my pants.

POLYMORPHONUCLEARLEUKOCYTE

Now here is a word you all ought to know.
How to pronounce it, well that's quite a show.
Just break up each part, now give it a try,
po-ly-morph-o-nuc-lear-leu-ko-cyte – oh my!

Now just what does it mean?
I had hoped you would ask.
Go get a dictionary,
now that is your task!

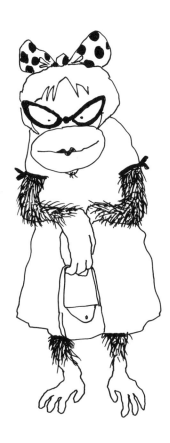

I'M NOT THE MONKEY'S UNCLE

If you're a monkey's uncle,
then who's the monkey's aunt?
I'm not a monkey's uncle,
but a gorilla's, I will grant.

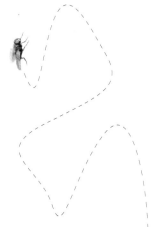

SLUSH

In the winter it gets snowy, when I go out to play.
And when it starts to warm up, near the end of day,

the snow gets wet and slushy and gathers in great piles.
I like to ball it up then and watch my sisters' smiles.

I knock the snow off trees, with snowballs made of slush.
I put my hands together and give that slush a crush.

All the girls go screaming,
as I chase them with snow.

They come back hard with snowballs,
and to my yard I go!

SNOW

Let it snow,
        let it snow,
            let it snow!
                Here we go,
                    here we go,
                        here we go!
                            When it's cold
                                and it's wet,
                                    we're not upset!
                                Here we go,
                                    let it snow,
                                        here we go!

IT'S SNOWING

It is snowing!
It is pouring!
I can't go out?
BUT THAT'S BORING!

Why not though?
Mom said so!
I said, "Please?"
She said, "NO!"

"Please, just in our yard?"
That's where I want to go.
But mom just stayed firm,
"I SAID NO! NO! NO! NO!"

It is just no use,
I guess I'm staying in!
That snow looks so good,
to be inside seems a sin.

But, I just broke my ankle,
and the rest of my leg.
So, it is no matter,
just how hard I might beg.

My mom's staying firm,
I will see no snow action.
Oh, well, it's hard to get up,
when you are stuck in traction!

I GOT MY BRACES TIGHTENED

I had to see the ortho.
He greeted me with pliers.
My brothers said it wouldn't hurt,
I knew they were both liars.

The ortho walked up to my chair,
and smiled his toothy grin.
He said, "Open up your mouth!"
He put his fingers in.

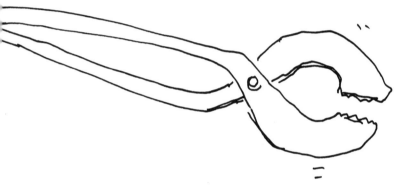

He twisted and he tightened.
It didn't feel too great.
I asked if he could stop it.
He said it was too late.

When I got home, I thumped my brothers,
on their arms, both left and right.
Though my mouth hurt really bad,
I bit them out of spite!

MY FEET SURE STINK

I pulled my shoes off quickly,
and then I held my breath.
My little brother yelled, "PEE-YOO!
Your feet smell just like DEATH!"

I sneered and growled at him,
he ran to Mom and cried.
"Mom, brother's feet sure stink
like cauliflower when it's fried."

I shoved my shoes back on so fast,
and laced them up real tight.
When Dad came in to my room,
he said, "Turn off your light!"

I nestled in my bed,
in my shoes I wiggled toes.
I pulled them off and kicked them out,
and pinched and held my nose.

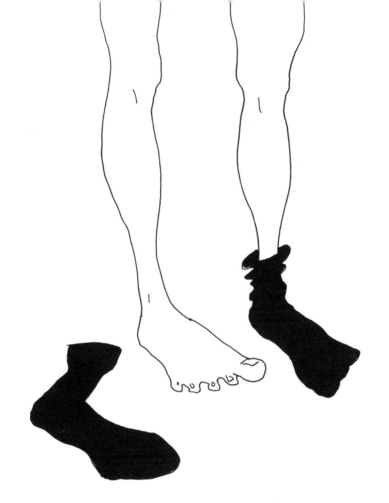

A NEST

While sweeping my porch
I heard a soft tweet.
I heard it again,
I walked to my seat.

Above my own head,
was a very small bird,
sitting up in his nest,
that's the tweeting I heard.

He'd used the bathroom,
while I sat beneath his nest.
Because now it is dripping,
down my forehead and my chest.

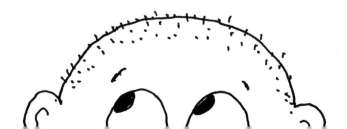

WHISTLE

My big brother always whistles.
He makes up most of his songs.
Now I want to learn to whistle.
Just why would that be wrong?

So I form my lips into a kiss,
in a pucker really tight.
I try and try and try some more,
with all my pucker might.

And when I finally get it,
I whistle then non-stop.
Until my jaw feels really sore,
and my lips begin to flop.

Now I whistle my own songs,
in the shower and on my bike.
It's hard not to whistle all the time.
It's something I just like!

WATERBOY (er, WATERPERSON)

I'm just too short to play,
and I don't weigh enough.
So I carry all the water,
oh, this job is really tough.

But someday, I will grow!
You all just wait and see!
I'll tackle and I'll jump!
When I'm tall like a tree!

A waterperson no more.
Oh yes, a star I'll be!
What is all that yelling?
The coach is mad at me.

Daydreaming gets me in trouble.
The players need their water.
Sometimes it is oh so tough,
to be the coach's daughter.

SHOWER DRAINS AND TOILETS

I'm afraid I might fall in,
when I'm taking a shower.
I'll get sucked in the toilet,
in the corner I just cower.

Near the door of the bathroom
and away from all the drains,
to go through the sewer pipes
would cause me some big pains.

SNACKS

Honey dipped ants,
big chocolate grubs,
I eat them in buckets,
I pour 'em in tubs.

I can't get enough,
of those bugs on my plate.
What? You haven't tried one?
Well do, they are great!

GIRL GERMS AND BOY GERMS

HIM -

When playing some tag,
I most often gag,
when a girl brushes close to my arm!

HER -

And I think it's just gross,
when a boy gets too close,
because they smell like a farm!

HIM -

Well, dolls are dorky,
and I don't like your dress.

HER -

Your opinions don't matter!
Boys are dumb, I confess!

HIM -

Girl Germs!

HER -

Boy Germs!

HIM/HER -

YOU STAY AWAY!
Oh, come on this is silly,
why don't we all play?

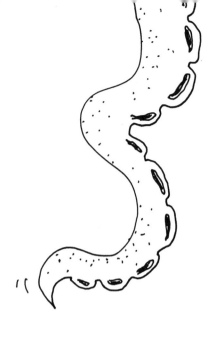

VAMPIRES AND MONSTERS

They creep and they lurk.
They're quite often berserk!
They suck on your neck and your arm.
They come out at night.
They're a terrible sight.
Especially when found in a swarm.

But, garlic some say,
will chase them away,
yet monsters eat garlic for snacks.
Stay away from that ghoul,
please don't be a fool,
or you're what a monster attacks!

But I found something neat,
that monsters like sweets!
They'll be your best friend if you share!
Give them gum and some candy,
they'll think you're so dandy,
no more of monsters you will be scared!

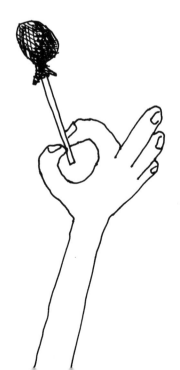

BAD DREAMS

Nightmares and ghoulies,
and scaries and BOOlies,
are stomping about in my mind.
I'm going to wake up, when my dream is all done.
It's make believe, I'm sure I will find.

SPIT

Oh, the wonder of spit, to try and explain,
would take a whole day and a half.
It's just fun to do, until it lands on your shoe,
but that makes all your friends laugh!

You can spit in the wind,
you can spit off a bridge,
you can spit anywhere, any day.
It's vulgar and crude,
and really quite rude,
but to spit is just fun, anyway!

Well, spit is a subject that's gross in a way,
it's something most often quite fun.
Spit isn't a good thing to talk about,
so that's all I'll say, I am done!

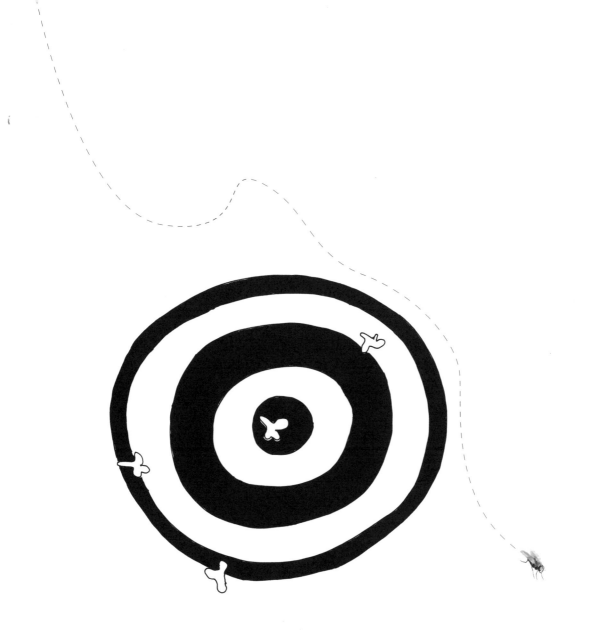

CLEAN YOUR ROOM

There are clothes all around,
something's spilled, running down,
the front of *your* dresser drawer.
Your bed is unmade,
looks like lemonade,
is so ancient it's stuck to your floor!

Did a hurricane hit,
that place where you sit?
Did a tornado pass by this room?
I'm surprised by this mess!
'Specially since we have guests!
Now go find a rag and a broom!

DOG HEAVEN

There've got to be bones and hydrants about,
for dogs to enjoy all the time.
To go for a walk, and there they can talk,
on hills meant for all dogs to climb.

Dog heaven must be great, I mean really first rate,
'cause dogs are the best of all pets!
There'll be food everywhere, and cats to chase there.
And no reason to have any vets!

Dog heaven must be big, so many places to dig!
There will be dogs of every old size!
They will jump and run fast, oh, it sounds like a blast!
And good dogs always win the first prize!

PEARLY GATES

St. Peter will be, standing, waiting for me.
But his wait might be longer than guessed.
When I go up there, I might wear underwear,
or show up in Momma's best dress.

A boy in a dress? Now why would that be?
Because I like to make people smile.
When they let me go in, they all will grin.
But I think I'll stay here for a while!

MY BELLY BUTTON COULD EAT ME

It lurks beneath my shirt,
it watches what I do!
One day my belly button,
will eat me, this is true.

MY TEDDY BEAR HABIT

I'm older than I should be,
to have a favorite Teddy.
But I just do, it's a fact,
and Teddy's name is Freddy.

MY BLANKIE

It's tattered and it's old.
It's seen a better day.
My blankie is my favorite thing,
I think it's quite okay.
I keep it in my pocket now,
it used to look so nice.
I love my favorite blankie,
so now I'll hug it twice!

TOILET PAPER ON MY FOOT

The bathroom stall was dark and wet,
but I just had to go.
I came out into the light,
and put on quite a show.

I walked around downtown,
with no idea why all the smiles.
And then a mean old lady,
pointed at my shoe, "Oh what a style!"

She cackled and she laughed aloud,
and showed bad manners too.
I looked right down and saw it,
toilet paper stuck upon my shoe.

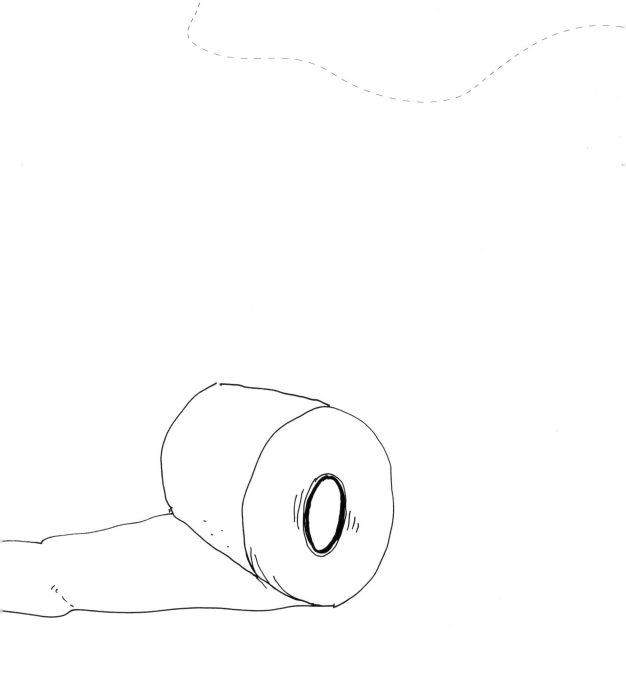

WARNING! WARNING!! WARNING!!!

THE FOLLOWING POEMS
ARE FOR TEACHERS ONLY!
KIDS WILL NOT LIKE THEM!
THEY ARE MOSTLY ABOUT
W R I T I N G !

YOU HAVE BEEN WARNED!

OH, SATURDAY'S A COMING!

School is boring!
Books are dumb!
I wish my favorite day would come!
It's homework, more work, papers to write,
Saturday seems so out of sight!

On Monday my week has just begun…
When Tuesday comes it's just not fun…
And Wednesday is the hump between…
When Thursday's here, I'm not as mean…

But Friday, oh boy, we're so near!
My mood just lifts, it comes quite clear,
Saturday's the best day of the week!
No papers to grade, no need to speak!

I lounge in bed and eat bon-bons,
and turn the television set back on.
I watch my favorite movies, too.
Come Sunday, I think of my "zoo."

My students will be back tomorrow.
A stack of papers to grade, OH MY SORROW!
It's back to school, OH YEAH! OH GREAT!
Well, Saturday's coming, I JUST CAN'T WAIT!

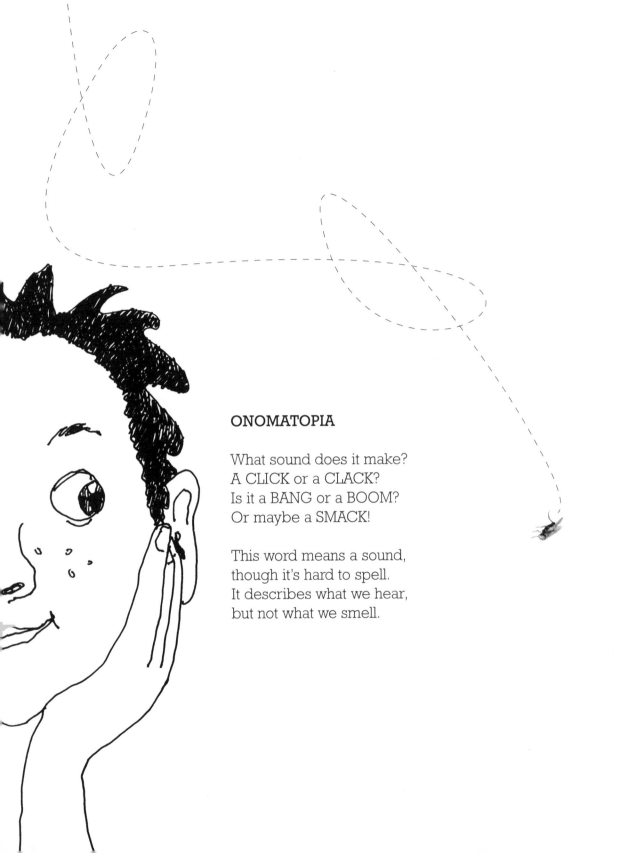

ONOMATOPIA

What sound does it make?
A CLICK or a CLACK?
Is it a BANG or a BOOM?
Or maybe a SMACK!

This word means a sound,
though it's hard to spell.
It describes what we hear,
but not what we smell.

ONOMATOLOGY

To form a word by hearing,
would describe this word I guess.
But it's so hard to say,
to you I must confess.

Like SMASH and BANG and others,
and then there is ACHOO!
These words are some to ponder,
CRASH and SMACK to name a few.

Add sound effects to your writing,
and your stories will be great!
As your ideas start a'buzzing,
they will all become first rate!

MY LITTLE BLACK BOOK

A place to store ideas,
until they turn to poems.
The fantastic or the funny,
all sorts of silly tomes.

'Neckties and gummy worms,'
'A pebble in your shoe,'
'A froggy in a boiling pot,'
plus things that I must do.

All these things are noted,
in the book I organize.
Silly things to write about,
the goofy and the wise.

My black book holds my best ideas,
and some that aren't so great.
I think I'm out of things to say.
But, wait, oh just you wait.

Go out and get a little book,
to write *YOUR* stories down.
It doesn't have to be black or little,
if you rather, large and brown.

Put down all of your ideas,
don't leave any of them out.
You never know what'll happen,
or what you'll write about!

WRITE TO A FRIEND

You have to send a letter
to your very "bestest" buddy.
You cannot think of what to say,
your brain's all turned to putty.

Just set your pencil down and think,
and ponder for awhile.
Soon you'll know just what to say,
to make your buddy smile.

Yes, soon a thought might come to you,
you'll maybe write it down.
You'll chew and chew and chew and chew,
and maybe even frown.

But then the words will come together,
for a friend a poem is born.
You'll stuff it in an envelope,
and send it in the morn.

REVISE THIS! REVISE THAT!

Revise this! Revise that!
I'm really getting mad!
All these changes to my stuff,
and my first draft wasn't bad!

But my teacher says to go back,
and check my spelling, too.
Some words I used were not the best,
some too many, some too few.

Why must I change my writing so?
Why revise, revise, revise?
And then the second time I do,
my teacher seems more wise.

They're getting so much better,
and making some more sense.
It's amazing how just one thing,
like a simple change in tense,

can make a story better,
can bring my words alive.
Thank you, teacher, for your work,
draft number fifty-five.

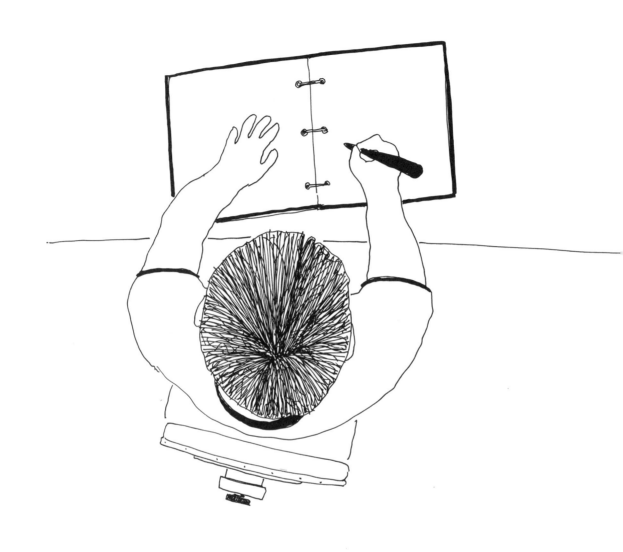

THIS POEM'S FOR YOU

Whenever I have some time,
I write my thoughts all down.
I write some just to laugh a lot,
I write some just to frown.

I hope you will like them,
these poems between us,
are just my silly thoughts.
So don't make a big fuss.

Sit down with a good book,
turn the pages slow or fast.
The stories you are reading,
will last and last and last.

Now, sit and write your own poems.
Just create them from your head.
Try reading to your brother,
or your sister in her bed.

If they giggle, it is funny.
If they cry, it may be sad.
Then read all of your new poems,
to your mom or to your dad.

But mostly just write them down,
and read them when alone.
It's amazing how happy you will be,
when reading your own poem.

WHILE IN CREATIVE WRITING CLASS

Boys like all the potty talk,
and girls just roll their eyes,
when we work all together,
but that's no big surprise.

There's romance and adventure,
and so much more to tell.
The boys like underwear jokes,
and things that really smell.

Yes, there is quite a difference,
when writing in a story.
But then there are some girls,
who write of guts and gory.

And some boys like romance,
and things that aren't so strange.
I guess we are most similar,
so we'll write in a big range.

A POEM

A poem can be a simple thing,
yet some are very deep.
Some will make you laugh and smile,
and some might make you weep.
A poem contains the mysteries,
of what we want to say.
You never know what kind of poem,
might come to you today.

THE SNOWBALL EFFECT

Snowballs are like ideas,
and thoughts all of your own.
From a little snowflake,
just look how it has grown.

They add up, it gets deeper,
the stories come to you.
You then can write a story
or maybe you'll write two.

"EYE LIK TWO RITE"

When I talk about editing,
I use this simple phrase.
You know exactly what I mean,
you can write it many ways.

But I used the wrong eye,
and then used the wrong two.
How can we make this sentence,
say what I really like to do?

Change the eye into an "I",
to the lik just add an e.
Try a to where the two is,
it's as easy as can be.

And a w in front of rite,
add a period on the end.
Or an exclamation mark will do,
how much you like it will depend.

Writing uses my imagination,
and I hope you'll get my clue.
Now my sentence says the same thing,
but it's much more clear for you.

That's clearly, "I like to write!"
Instead of, "Eye lik two rite,"
It's just important to be clear,
revising makes it tight!

WHATEVER COMES TO MIND FIRST

You might have guessed by now,
no subject is too taboo.
There are so many ways to say,
the things that you want to.

Now go and get your pencil,
and draw yourself a thing.
Then set to words your story,
and let your words just ring.

Write what comes to your mind first,
don't worry if it's dumb.
From one small word and sentence,
will your own stories then come!

INDEX

THE END (A NOTE FROM MATOTT AND WOODS)

"THE END" IS HOW STORIES OFTEN FINISH.
BUT THIS BOOK HAS MANY TALES.
AND SO INSTEAD OF "THE END",
WHY DON'T YOU SEND US MAIL?

GIVE US SUBJECTS FOR OUR NEXT BOOK,
AND IF WE PICK YOUR SUBJECT OUT,
WE'LL PUT YOUR NAME BESIDE IT,
NOW, WON'T THAT MAKE YOU SHOUT?

"HOORAY FOR MY IDEA,
IT GOT PICKED FOR THE NEXT BOOK!
BUT I WON'T GET ANY ROYALTIES...
WOW, THEIR PUBLISHER'S A CROOK!"

Just kidding about the crook part, sadly not kidding about the lack of royalties for naming a poem, the only gratuity you will receive is the knowledge that your idea was used. If you have an idea for a quip for Matott and Wood's next anthology of poems called *Chocolate Covered Frog Legs*, please send your ideas to:

Clove Publications, Inc.
CHOCOLATE FROGS
P.O. Box 261183
Littleton, CO 80163